1 MONTH OF
FREE
READING

at

www.ForgottenBooks.com

By purchasing this book you are eligible for one month membership to ForgottenBooks.com, giving you unlimited access to our entire collection of over 1,000,000 titles via our web site and mobile apps.

To claim your free month visit:

www.forgottenbooks.com/free18487

ISBN 978-0-484-58369-5
PIBN 10018487

AN UNVESTED SISTER

RECOLLECTIONS OF

MARY WILTSE

NEW-YORK, JAMES POTT & CO. 1891

248
W75 m

Those who knew Mary Wiltse intimately will naturally turn to the sketch "An Unvested Sister," which gives its title to this little book. But there are others, doubtless, into whose hands these further Recollections may fall, who will welcome a more detailed account of her life.

It will be noticed in reading these pages that the writer has avoided describing Miss Wiltse's work as institutional, and in so doing he has but reflected her own mind. As one has written, whose relations to that work give his words peculiar weight: "She proved how an institution could be rescued from the spirit of institutionalism, by the glow of a personal enthusiasm."

This was evidenced particularly in the way she multiplied her influence beyond the four walls of the Nursery by using the confidence and affection of the children as a means of reaching the homes in which they lived. Such multiplication of influence told heavily upon her. Had she chosen a career extensive in point of time, by husbanding her interests for her immediate surroundings, rather than one intensive in point of unselfish and unprovincial devotion, her earthly life, one cannot doubt, might have been prolonged. But one may well question if in that case it would have had more than a superficial potency.

The life whose story quickens and thrills us most, must ever be that whose supremest note is sacrifice.

GEORGE H. BOTTOME.

GRACE HOUSE, EASTER, 1891.

Behold I and the children
which God hath given me.

I.

LIFE AT SING SING.

MARY WILTSE, the third daughter of Robert Wiltse and his wife, Mary Romeyn Bard, was born at Sing Sing, on the Hudson, on Easter Sunday, 1843; and her life, until, in 1879, she came to New York, was passed almost wholly in the town of her birth. She was native to that region which the pen of Irving has immortalized, and the natural magic clinging to its surroundings never ceased to have fascination for her. It was doubtless the infinite variety of the associations of these early years that gave rise to the wish long after, when Grace House-by-the-Sea became overcrowded, that a real *country* home could be found for "her" children.

Her mother tells a story of her very young childhood which those who knew her in her later life will find characteristic. It happened when she was only seven years old that she made her first visit away from Sing Sing. She had been taken to spend a few days with the family of Dr. Berrian, then Rector of Trinity Church, New-York, with whom she was a great pet. At the end of two days she grew sick with longing for her country home, and, without saying a word to any one, managed in some mysterious way to get to the station, and on the train. The train had hardly started when she found she had lost her purse; but, when the conductor came to collect her fare, she said, with perfect assurance: "I've lost my money, but I'm Robert Wiltse's daughter."

Of course, says her mother, the little thing was taken care of, and, to the astonishment of the home circle, walked in upon them an hour later, alone and unattended, with her small package under her arm!

The fearlessness that made her remarkable then was but intensified as she grew older. The woman who, as a child, did not dread to take this solitary journey, went many a dark night alone through some of the worst haunts of the great city, in search of this or that one, who, but for her, had been lost indeed.

She was the favorite of her father, who delighted to "draw her out," greatly relishing and repeating her quaint sayings. Full of humor always, and keenly alive to the ludicrous side of things, her childhood was especially happy, and the intense hopefulness with which she looked out upon life, no after change of sorrow and trial could wholly dispel. If there was one virtue whose presence in her, under circumstances however trying, impressed most deeply her friends of later years, it was this buoyant optimism, the determination to find, if such was to be found, the bright side. Instances shall illustrate this for us later on; but the woman was so strongly prophesied in the child, that one is tempted to anticipate what really belongs to her matured life.

When Mary was a very young girl a favorite cousin left home to study in New-York, and her correspondence with him, always conducted in rhyme, showed a real talent for versification. She was, as well, an excellent musician, and, until the time she entered wholly into church work, had a large class of pupils in music. In after years she deeply regretted that she

had not the time to "keep up her music";
but never, when she could help it, would
she miss playing for the children in the
Nursery at the morning office, or at the
Chantry services in the afternoon.

Her studies during her school-days were
in the main carried on at home under the
direction of governesses, and there is no
evidence that her bent of mind at this
time in any way gave hint of the character of the work she was afterwards to
undertake. It was in her nineteenth year
that she had her first experience in nurs-
ing the sick, and with that experience her
life took on a certain distinction it had not
possessed before. Her younger sisters had
been attacked with scarlet fever, and in
the town itself no one could be found
willing to help in the care of them.
Whereupon Mary took the youngest, then
a baby, to her own room, watched it
night and day with an attention that

never faltered, and brought it through the crisis. The disposition thus manifested was taxed again and again in the years that followed. At this time she was a young woman of extraordinary strength of body and acuteness of mind. Often, after a long day spent at teaching, she would walk, however inclement the weather, any distance to carry nourishment to the sick poor. A group of incidents, which might easily be added to, go to show how absorbing such work became to her.

There was then in existence in Sing Sing a miserable little alley, the haunt of the vicious and degraded, and the scene of frequent drunken brawls. Into this place no respectable person cared to venture, and here it was that a poor woman, Ellen ——, lay dying of consumption. Her home was a little shanty composed of two rooms. That in which Ellen lay was destitute of even a bed, and she herself was laid on a heap of rags in the corner. At the time Mary heard of her, Ellen's husband, as well as her father and mother, were drunkards of the worst type, indifferent, and at times positively cruel to the dying girl. Not a hand had been raised to alleviate her misery until Mary came. She immediately procured all the necessary comforts for the woman, and, as money could not hire help to clean the rooms, scrubbed the wall, floor, and every nook and corner of the place herself. One of her daily duties was to go each morning, bathe the sufferer, freshen the bed, and, as best she might, keep the rooms clean, preparing and taking to the dark alley all the nourishment the invalid needed. Ellen lingered for months, but never during the hot or cold weather did Mary neglect her charge. Many a bitter winter's evening she went quietly from a merrymaking in her own home to pass the night by Ellen's bedside, and protect her from the brutal attacks of drunken husband and parents. Mary saw that her charge was baptized and confirmed, and when Ellen died it was in a faith cheered and encouraged by the love of her friend. The father died not long after, but the husband reformed, and is now a respectable mechanic. Two years ago the mother came to see Miss Wiltse, told her what a comfortable home she now had, and that every day of her life she ceased not to pray for her who had been so good to her daughter, and had taught the mother how to lead a Christian life.

It happened once during an epidemic of scarlet fever in the lower quarter of the town that one poor family was left utterly destitute, no one daring to venture near them. Mary, hearing of the case, at once went to them, and took up her quarters in the wretched hovel for days, caring for the sick until they were able to care for themselves.

But her work was by no means confined to the poor. It was before the days of trained nurses, and requisition was only too often made on her unfailing skill and unflagging spirits. At one time she gave up all other work for three months to watch by the bedside of a friend dying of a most painful and trying disease. Upon the end of this protracted vigil she was utterly broken down, even her strong constitution being unable to bear the extraordinary burdens she put upon it in the service of others.

One more instance of the many we might quote: In 18—, a boys' school at Sing Sing was to be moved away in the middle of the term. On the eve of starting one of the students was taken ill with malignant typhoid fever, and all hotels and lodging-houses refused to give him shelter. The family of the principal, who were friends of Mary, begged her to take him, and, with her mother's permission, she brought him to her home. She alone nursed him through three days of frightful illness, attended by severe convulsions. At the end of the third day, just at sunset, he passed away peacefully in her arms.

It will be seen from such instances how high a place she could have gained for herself as a trained nurse, had her life work chanced to take that direction. But the experience of these early years proved of immense help and value to her in her New-York life.

By no means did she, for the sake of work extra-parochial, neglect her own church. It is no less than astonishing that she was able to do not only so much for the church, or so much for cases similar to those to which we have referred, but that she found time and strength to meet the claims made upon her from both sources at the same time. She loved her Communion with that same eager devotion which had led her father to begin and see completed the first Episcopal church edifice in Sing Sing. For many years, and until his death, Robert Wiltse was senior warden of St. Paul's, and the mantle of unflagging zeal in its service fell at his death upon his daughter. One who knew her well in those days writes: "I cannot help thinking that, with all the earnest, faithful labor which has been devoted to the church, such lives as hers are rare. There is one kind of heroism which leads the charge in the fight and heads the forlorn hope which storms the fortress, but there is another, and, doubtless, a nobler heroism, which is not born of the battle, but which hides itself from the world, and finds its field in the quiet daily life of humanity. Such heroism she had, and those of us who were daily witnesses of it will not fail to take its lessons to our hearts." What the parish of St. Paul's, and what its rector and her unfailing friend, Dr. Helm, would have done without her, it is difficult to imagine. At a time when peculiar difficulties and dissensions arose, Mary remained loyal to him, and to the church of her childhood. The division resulting in the forming of a new parish in no way affected her eager zeal in behalf of the older organization, but rather intensified it. "It is safe to say," writes a friend, "that in the parish labors her counsel and assistance were alike sought and always given, without, however, the slightest assumption on her part of authority or dictation."

How like an echo of these words is the testimony of the rector of Grace Parish, after her death: "The clergy of the parish counted on her help as if she had been one of their own order." With what gratitude would that older friend, had he been living, have witnessed the truth of this tribute. Under Dr. Helm her spiritual life quickened, and grew, and broke into flower. She never forgot her debt to him, and her loving loyalty to all he loved and cherished never wavered. She was a voluntary parish visitor, and the mainstay of what would have been, but for her, a run-down and deserted Sunday-school. Again and again did she take from her own income, which was by no means large, money to defray expenses for the poor which otherwise, because of an empty treasury, could not have been met. "At one time," writes one of her sisters who was with her in the Sunday-school, "she swept and dusted the church, and often, in the absence of the sexton, have known her to mount up into the belfry and ring the bell for service. She made a full set of ecclesiastical hangings and colors for the different seasons, and, having raised money to recarpet the church, helped to lay it herself. All this, of course, was at the time when the church she had so dearly loved was struggling to live." Writes the friend from whom I have already quoted: "Those who were of that congregation while she was a member of it cannot fail to recall her patience, skill, and efficiency in the department for which she seemed peculiarly fitted—the management and training of young children. She taught the infant class so long and so successfully that to us she seems to be identified with it, and in our thoughts of her we always picture her as she sat, surrounded by the little ones, holding their unwavering attention to their work. There was no more pleasant sight at the annual Christmas festival than the infant class, with its teacher at its head, marching to its place, singing its triumphant hymn, 'Jerusalem the Golden.' The children's love for her was boundless, and their impatience whenever she was absent amusingly frank. On one occasion, having to leave town, she gave the class in charge of a younger sister. Upon her return the children exclaimed: 'Oh, we are glad you are back; we had a teacher *who knew nothing!*' "

Mary was intimate with the family of every child in the Sunday-school, as well as those represented by the particular class of which she had charge. She came, therefore, in contact with some of the older children, and gained an influence over them which passing years only deepened. Said a woman to one of her sisters, not long ago: " My boy owes his strong sense of right to the influence and love Miss Mary gave out to him." And that is but one of many like testimonies loving hearts were eager to offer as tributes of affection to "Miss Mary's" memory. It was by that title she came to be best known; a title which, ere long, secured her instant access to any quarter, however dubious, of her native village, and one which, after the lapse of years, calls up to the mind of many a grateful heart recollections of kindly words and generous deeds. Thus, in the town of her childhood and young womanhood, did she pass her days. She was in no sense a recluse. The world to her was indeed "no blot nor blank." But, as the claims upon her grew heavier, either from parochial or extra-parochial sources, what time she had to spare was given up, almost entirely, to meeting them. If trial and sorrow came to her, they were bravely borne. Then, as ever, she found relief by throwing herself with passionate eagerness into the lives of those about her, giving freely and unstintingly the best that was in her, of faith, courage, and love. If the end had come then, had her life been associated with no more than that which her unwearied hands had accomplished in the village of her birth, its memory would still be a source of inspiration to those who knew her. It falls to the lot of but few to do what she had already done when, in 1879, she left Sing Sing to take up a work of large possibilities, which she was destined nobly to realize and improve.

II

LIFE AT THE DAY NURSERY.

IN the note of the Rector,[1] introductory to the Year-Book of Grace Parish of 1877, there is mention made of a house in East 13th Street, which was to meet various needs, one of which was a Day Nursery. "I am," he said, "anxious to open a *crèche* where working women may leave their children during working hours, and where at such times they may be wisely and kindly cared for." It was on the 4th of March in the following year that this Day Nursery was opened. Those who know

[1] Rt. Rev. Henry C. Potter, then Rector of Grace Church.

the Nursery as it is to-day will be amused
to hear that one of the first comments entered in the visitors' book was to the
effect that everything seemed promising
save the absence of the children — *where
are they?* It seems a long time indeed
since any such remark could be made!
For a year and a half from the time of
opening, the managers of the new char-
ity struggled unsuccessfully with the
problem how to find the right superintendent for the place. Miss Wiltse's con-
sent to undertake the work solved it finally
for them. One who was present at her
first interview with the Rector and the
managers of the Nursery has said how
amazed she was to learn afterwards that
she who seemed no more than a young
girl was in her thirty-seventh year. To
the last she impressed those who knew
her as being so much younger than she
really was. Her quick humor, her irre-

pressible vitality, her clear, fearless, blue eyes, and, above all, her hair, in which never a thread of white showed for all her labors, all these combined to deceive even her intimate friends. Well, indeed, for her that through the years of her work she could carry a young heart, and undaunted courage, for they were sorely needed.

A word ought to be said at the outset as to the method Miss Wiltse adopted in the carrying on and developing of her work.

A dear friend of hers, who knew and valued her devotion as few could, said, in speaking upon this question of method: "There are two ways such a work might be managed. Regard it wholly in the light of an institution, all co-workers as parts of a machine, and you can doubtless save yourself much labor and the immediate object aimed at, the caring for the children during the day, be attained. But this Mary

Wiltse did not do. She looked on the Nursery as a home: each inmate, child, servant, or nurse, part of her immediate care. Consequently she was always giving out of her own vitality in a thousand ways. *She would take indifferent material into her household and make it good.* This a manager of an ordinary institution would not take the trouble to do. She would show the deepest personal interest in the families represented by the children in the *crèche*, and, above all, she made it her daily and devout duty to impress and mold as best she might the lives of those about her with her own strong and steadfast faith."

There was nothing at this time too hard for her unimpaired health and spirits. She used to relate with great glee how one morning stealing off in the gray dawn of a winter's day to open the Nursery at six, she had been discovered by an early riser at the rectory and ordered back to her rooms. This had gone on for some time, and there was no certainty then, as, indeed, ever afterwards, that she would learn how to husband her resources, and not to be spendthrift with her strength. But the work had to be done, she used to say, and when it came to getting help, that was about as difficult as anything else. What the work soon became to her the following letter will show:

I was so glad this evening to receive your letter. When it came I was having a very exciting conversation with —— in regard to the old story of the Orphan Asylum. He had just come from the city where he had seen his aunt (who is the matron), and found her determined to leave her position the first of the month. He went to see the lady managers, of course without my knowledge, for I had not even seen him. He argued the matter very strongly, and laughed at the idea that I would not soon become as much attached to the work there as I am to the Nursery. I told him that it could not be. My own work in all its different bearings was very dear to me, and even the extra $300 a year offered no inducement, as I am not doing my work for money. My friends are all anxious for me to take it.

At this time the work was being carried on under many disadvantages. The quarters devoted to the Nursery were painfully limited. Part of the house was given over to a Free Library (afterwards developed into the New-York Free Circulating Library), and certain rooms were assigned for the use of one of the assistant ministers. But, cramped as the Nursery was for proper accommodation, the attendance day by day was proportionally large nevertheless. The interest in her work which the letter just quoted betrays, was but deepened and intensified with the opening of the present "Grace Memorial House." The building 94 and 96 Fourth Avenue was the gift of the Hon. Levi P. Morton, a parishioner of Grace Church, in memory of his wife Lucy Kimball. The formal opening did not take place before the spring of 1883, but long before that the eager superintendent had moved in, "to the disgust of the workmen," she said laughingly years afterwards.

It is safe to say that neither the giver nor the architect watched the progress of the building more keenly than its future superintendent. Whenever she could spare the time she hovered about the workmen, giving suggestions as to what was most necessary to be done, and when the building was finally completed a more grateful and satisfied woman could not be found. It would be difficult certainly to find a building whose interior is so admirably adapted for its particular use, as is its exterior to charm and delight the eye. The Nursery in its new quarters accommodated in all nearly ninety children, and at times the number overran that limit. The *crèche* for the youngest children and babies ; the school-room where the little ones from five years of age and upwards were gathered ; the children who were sent to day school, returning for their dinners, and remaining, after school was out, until six or seven — these may stand as representing the three divisions of the work of the Nursery proper. A number of the girls who had been brought as young children to the Nursery remained for years with Miss Wiltse, taking some position of helpfulness in the home as soon as they were old enough to do so. No blood relationship could have stimulated a deeper interest in the welfare of those associated with her in her work than that which softened and mellowed all Miss Wiltse's intercourse with the servants in her household. She was a living rebuke to anything like idleness. She would put her hand to any sort of work when emergency demanded, and from the hour she rose in the morning, usually before seven, until, twelve hours later, the last child had left the house, she never rested save at her meals. When it is remembered that until the break came she used to spend many of her evenings in the families of the children she had cared for in the day time, it is not to be wondered at that her prayer that " she might not rust out" was granted.

Mary's satisfaction in the new home is pictured in the following letter to a friend:

Last evening we had the first christening in the oratory. Do you remember the tiny little baby? I have had her in the Nursery since she was ten days old. Her mother and father wanted to have her baptized here, and as they felt they owed everything to this house they named her for me, and wished that I should be her godmother, which I really do not fancy, as I have nearly one hundred godchildren all over the universe now. As they speak no English Mr. Woolsey baptized her, using the German service. It was a very pretty sight. We had the corona lighted, which made the room brilliant, and we had quite a congregation. The baby was lovely and she crowed through the baptism as if she knew it all. We are having very interesting services now; for several days every seat has been filled ; and the children are so reverent. God grant it may bring a blessing to us all. . . . To-day they have finished putting the window in the oratory. It is very lovely. I cannot tell you how delighted I was this evening. The children knew nothing about it, so when I opened the doors it was a complete surprise. I did not say a word, but after looking at it a while they exclaimed as if with one voice, "Why, that is the Saviour calling the little children to him ! "

It was her habit during the earlier years of her work to keep a journal with a detailed account of the children brought into the Nursery. From that journal the abstracts given below are taken. As years went on and her work grew wider and more engrossing, she found it almost impossible to keep up with the record, and she always regretted that there were no entries later than 1886. "I hope sometime," she said once, "to fill in the more important cases from memory," but that time never came. These extracts are selected to show how varied were the claims made upon her interest and sympathy by those with whom the children brought her into contact. Under the date of November, 1881, there appears this entry:

GEORGIANA B. Three months old. English. Brought to the Nursery in November. The child was taken out of compassion for her mother who was trying very hard to make a living. The husband, who pretended to be a "Reformed Catholic" preacher, had deserted her after obtaining all the money that she had, leaving her with a baby only a few weeks old. The poor little thing was very delicate, owing to exposure and want of care, and, after a few months' struggle, was taken to Paradise December 20, 1881. The mother having no friends, sent for me and I was with her through all her trouble.

In October of that same year a child of Irish parentage was brought to the Nursery, the story of whose death is indescribably sad :

The mother (the record says) was a very dissipated woman and grossly neglected the baby, many times falling with it in the street on her way to the Nursery. Many attempts were made to find a home for it, and all unsuccessful owing to the baby's age. The father patiently tried to induce his wife to do better, and they met several times at the Nursery trying to reconcile matters, but she went from bad to worse, pawning even their household comforts. The poor baby was suffering in the winter with a severe cold and cried whenever taken from the Nursery at night. She died very suddenly on December 26, 1882. On going to the room that morning I found the mother in a drunken stupor on the floor, *and the child lying on a table where it had been dead for several hours.* I washed and dressed the dear little lamb, thankful that the Good Shepherd had taken her into his own care.

No case that ever came under her notice made such a deep and lasting impression upon her as did the following. Her friends can never forget her own description of what the bare facts as she recorded them in the journal can but faintly recall.

"EDDIE and IVAN G. Twins. Four years old. English. Entered the Nursery December, 1882. The mother was very peculiar and reticent, and hard in her every action and word. The children were bright, intelligent little fellows, only wanting love and tenderness to bring them out. . . . In March, 1883, Eddie was taken suddenly ill with croup. The children had never been baptized, the mother strongly objecting, but when there was no chance for the boy's life, Rev. Mr. Nelson at my request, and in despite of her remonstrances, baptized both children, she refusing to witness it. Within a week they were both taken, and her rebellious, wicked spirit was something dreadful to witness. She left the Nursery with almost a curse upon her lips. One year from that time she came back and asked to see me. She said she was a different woman and could see the wisdom and love of God in taking the children from her. It was found she was suffering with cancer, and, through the kindness of Mrs. Winthrop, her board was paid at the hospital for five months. She suffered very patiently and died a happy, resigned Christian. She had no relatives or friends in this country, and turned to me with the fondness and confidence of a child. She was buried by the side of her little ones, Rev. Mr. Young reading the service, Lizzie Grueber and I alone present.

The poor sufferer, in her gratitude to Miss Wiltse, willed to her all that she had in the world, *a lot in Evergreen Cemetery*.

Two more extracts must suffice to illustrate the value of her work, and the bitter need that a great city has of souls such as hers to humanize, to say nothing of Christianizing, it :

CATHERINE S. Italian. Entered the Nursery 1882. Found in the street asleep on the curbstone by the side of a peanut stand kept by her mother. The beauty of the child, as well as its wretched condition, caused an investigation. They slept in a miserable, damp basement, and the food given the child day by day consisted of stale fruit and peanuts. She was brought daily to the Nursery, and, with good food and comfortable clothing, soon became strong and well.

EDITH J. Twenty months. American Protestant. Entered Nursery September, 1884. The mother is a refined woman, well brought up, but married against her parents' wishes. She came to us in February of 1886, with a young babe of five weeks old in her arms, and told us that her husband had gone off with another woman and refused to come back. From her own story, I found they had both been to blame; so, after talking with both of them, advised them to try and do better, and take care of the children. I sent the husband to Dr. Huntington, who urged him to sign the pledge, and, with many promises, they began again, and at last accounts are doing well.

Her strong common sense comes out in clear outline in this last. She was ready enough to sympathize when she had plain before her eyes both sides of the question. She did not commit her feelings at first hearing of complaints and reproaches, all too common, made against the cruelties of their husbands by broken-hearted women. The world that opened before her day by day was a world of exceeding sadness and gloom, and had she not been thus wise in the husbanding of her sympathies for the proper moment, her spirit would have broken utterly. How many there are, into whose hands the record of such a life may fall, who cannot realize how complex and awful are the conditions of life existent in their midst, of which they are so helplessly ignorant. Day by day, month by month, year by year, to attempt into this gloom to throw a stream of pure, clear light; such was Mary Wiltse's work.

But by no means was her life devoid of sunshine and joy; nor did her constant contact with the "seamy side" of things result in embittering her own nature, or shadowing her intense faith. To those privileged to be her intimates, nothing could recall more instantly her bright, serene spirit, than the mention of that "back parlor," which served as dining and reception room alike. Here, especially on winter's evenings, in the later years of her life, she used to be found, surrounded by a multitude of pictures of children; and, if the hour was early, attended by, and engrossed in "Beatrice" and "Tommy"; children, these, of two helpers in the household, and who were, therefore, privileged persons indeed, having their home, with their mothers, in the Nursery.

Until these young people had been packed off to bed, it was next to useless to attempt to engage her attention upon any subject not immediately relating to them. But, once away, if one needed encouragement and aid, how instantly what I have called her buoyant optimism came into play. Her friends have sat fascinated many a time, as she told of some peculiarly hard experience through which she had gone, and out of which, for all its dubiousness, had come victorious. *"What,"* she used to say, *" can you expect of these poor things, when you see the way they have to live?"* And this clearsighted faculty of what one may call " relativity," never allowed her to lose heart.

Fond as she had been in her home of the society of her friends, she lived her life in New-York in many ways alone. She rarely made visits, save now and then for a few hours at her home in Sing Sing. Her work during the day tired her so completely, that at night she craved only the rest and peace of her little parlor. In the early years of her work, before she was in any way conscious of what weariness and physical depression meant, she gave herself no time to make friends other than those connected with the Nursery itself.

Later on her one and only aim was to do as much work as she could force herself to do, and consequently she did not care to seek interests outside, which would have brought new responsibilities. It was a mistake doubtless. There were many in that parish to whose activities her work gave distinction and color, who knew her but by name and would gladly have known her better. Hers was a life of such large outline, it seems a pity it was lived so much in seclusion. But it was not alone her fault that with so few was she intimately acquainted. It was owing in part to the peculiar conditions characteristic of a great city church, which make it, unhappily, so often possible for its workers to be hardly known to the majority of the members of the parish itself.

But with that little circle of friends of which she was the center, her memory is in no sense associated with things sad and depressing. "It is as if a bright light had gone out," said one of them at her death, a saying hardly in accord with a melancholy disposition. I dwell on this because of the fear that the record of the character of the work she did may lead one to think she herself caught its reflection. But no one ever had more genuine love of fun and humor to the very day of her death than she. A friend used to read her certain delightful "Bab Ballads," and the very last note received from her was a request to loan her his copy. "The verses keep running in my head and I cannot recall them exactly; do send it up." Books of a nature sad and depressing she abhorred. One sees too many sad things in real life, she used to say. In the face of much in her work that was discouraging and seemingly hopeless, the power to preserve a bright, sunny disposition must have been the result of struggle. She once warned a young clergyman, who, at the beginning of his ministry, was complaining to her of the heartless ingratitude of a certain "case" he had helped, of the temptation besetting him to harden his sympathies. She instanced her own experience to prove how mechanical and cold would her work have become had she not managed to overcome that temptation in herself. How signal and complete was her victory, those familiar with her methods and work can testify. Her lightheartedness was never a synonym for a shallow feeling or an indifferent spirit. She simply possessed in equal measure the ability to weep with them that wept, and to rejoice with them that rejoiced.

If she was occasionally subject to fits of depression there was always at hand an unfailing remedy. The writer remembers so well finding her one evening utterly broken down, as she seemed, over a case of peculiar sadness.   Added to that, some kindly disposed but ill advised critic, whose knowledge of all such work as hers was as great in theory as conspicuously lacking in practice, had chanced upon her when she needed sympathy most, and left her sorrowing and hurt.   But suddenly, like a gleam of light out of a dark cloud, her face brightened and broke into laughter as she recalled a comical remark of one of the children.   The transition was so sudden, that it left on the mind of her friend an impression not soon to be forgotten.   Yes, the supreme joy of her life was with and in the presence of the children.   They had nothing to give her but their love ; but that they gave her without stint.

Her one idea was to make the Nursery identical in their minds with all that was bright, and happy, and pure.   With the opening of the Summer Home at Far Rockaway in the same year that saw the

Memorial House completed, she began to have the children with her the " year round," and she charged herself with the responsibility for their bringing up in a way that most of their mothers might have imitated with good results. Her work here, especially among the younger children, buoyed up rather than taxed her energies. At least they were not ungrateful, and they responded to her loving efforts, and that in itself was infinite satisfaction.

Under date of August 12, 1883, she wrote to Mrs. Bowdoin:

How delighted you would be to see the children so well and happy. It is remarkable to think that they are taken away from their mothers and don't seem to mind it, but are so contented. Now I have gone through all the hard and unpleasant work of moving into and getting in order two new, unfinished houses, and the thought cannot but come to me, how long shall I be spared to see the fruit of all the hours of toil and anxious care ? I only pray for strength for my work and then I will be satisfied.

The best evidence that she made the Nursery a home indeed for the children, an extract from a letter of its physician, Dr. Nelson Henry, will show:

The attachment of the children to Miss Wiltse (he wrote) has been universal and always noticeable; and upon my visit to the houses of some very sick children they have always been most anxious to return to the Nursery. On two occasions, when the little ones became delirious, their mother informed me they would frequently cry out to be taken to Miss Wiltse.

To the mind of the writer the one thing that distinguished her work from other similar attempts was the remarkable and peculiar religious emphasis she attached to it. She was an earnest and devoted churchwoman, her early years at Sing Sing testified to that, but never was there woman similarly placed who had less of cant, general and particular, characterizing her teaching.

Her exposition of the collects and prayers, so simply and directly illustrated that the youngest of the little auditory could catch her meaning, was in itself a liberal education.

I have said she hated cant. She was called one day to see one of the youngest children lying at death's door. When she arrived, the poor thing was being put through a catechism as to her soul's condition, by a Bible Reader in the district. Mary stood it as long as she could, but finally her indignation boiled over, and she very decidedly made known to the well-intentioned but foolish woman that her presence was no longer required, and she would be responsible for the child.

The pride with which the older children took part in the Easter and Christmas festivals in the church was a sufficient testimony to the loving interest her teaching inspired in things good and true. How breathlessly still used the great school to become when the " Nursery choir" stood up to say, in place of the lesson, the Gospel for the Feast; or sang their Christmas hymn,

Holy night, peaceful night;
All is calm, all is bright.

The subject of death was a difficult one for explanation, and her letters throw light on her method of dealing with it. Under date of July 26, 1885, she writes to a friend:

My letter, you see, came to a standstill. The poor baby died Sunday night, at midnight, after hours of intense suffering. We buried him here yesterday afternoon. Mr. Nelson came down and we had a lovely service, the children all responding and singing. The baby, covered with flowers, and lying in his cradle, made a beautiful picture, even with death in the midst. I was entirely worn out yesterday, as I had held the little fellow through many hard convulsions for seven hours.

"I do not want," she used to say, "the children to have a sad impression of death." She taught, as of course she had always to teach, by illustration and parable. The future world was to the little ones the "Nursery in Paradise." Surely, no other picture could have given them a better idea of what happiness was in store for their brothers and sisters who had been, like early flowers, gathered in.

"I really feel sometimes," she said once, "that in trying to make the hereafter understandable to the children, I have almost materialized it for myself." But however she conceived it, it was something never out of her mind, something in which her faith struck but deeper and more vital roots, as the years went by. As late as February of 1890, she wrote these words: "Whatever happens to my babies, I know they are mine still, and I always think of them as a happy little family waiting and watching for the rest of us to come."

The following letters, written from Far Rockaway, give a glimpse of her work there, with its mingled sorrow and joy. During the months when the city house was open, she rarely wrote of her work, the friend upon whose love and sympathy she particularly relied seeing her almost daily. At the sea, however, she was quite alone, and of the few letters available almost all were written from Far Rockaway.

AUGUST 17TH.

I have Mrs. N. down here now. You remember she is the Frenchwoman who lost her two children a few weeks ago. She was so crushed and heart-broken, and so very ill herself, that it seemed as though there would never be any relief for her. She came down a week ago, with the only remaining little one, and it is a comfort to see what the change has done for her. She is more cheerful, and begins to see her way through the darkness which has surrounded her. This summer I have had several persons here in the same condition, suffering with poverty, ill health, and sorrow. They are the ones that it gladdens my heart to have about me, and to work for. The entire change in their outer life has a perceptible influence on the inner, and lifts their hearts as well as their hands.

AUGUST 10, 1884.

I find I must give up going to church, when I have such a houseful. Sunday is really a very hard day. The husbands, uncles, cousins and aunts of all these people come down to visit them, and, to preserve any kind of order, I must be right here. . . . The child I brought down four weeks ago, whom everybody thought was sure to die, I shall send home to-morrow, so fat his waists won't fit him! He is the picture of health, though when he came he was in a bad condition. I just watched his diet, and took the greatest care of him in every way, and now he is well. . . . (Sunday, P. M.) We have had a great excitement here. We had a shock of earthquake, and a more terrified household you cannot imagine. I was sitting on the piazza with a baby on my lap, and I really thought we were all gone.

The following letter will provoke a smile on the part of those who remember how indissolubly wedded to her work she was. But at times even her splendid spirits broke down, and more than once it happened at such a crisis that tempting offers to initiate similar work elsewhere were made her. A woman of such intense individuality could not fail to have sharp critics, whose attitude hurt her more, and cut more deeply into her nature, than all her burdens, whether voluntarily assumed or imposed by others. It was at such a time that she wrote to her friend.

SEPTEMBER 1, 1885.

I am only going to write you a line, for I am so miserable and dull this morning, I only wish I were home. This sudden change in the weather has given me a cold which seems to have settled in my left side and I have suffered very much since Sunday. Dr. —— and his wife were here yesterday ; and he would be only too glad if I would go to ——. As soon as I go back to the city I intend to tell —— the reason that I want to give up my work. While it might break my heart to give up a work which has been so dear to me, I must consider myself a little.

The very last thing she ever did, it may safely be said, was to "consider herself," and though the offer then made was afterwards renewed, she declined it, as it was felt she would when the matter came to a decision. One lady deeply interested in her work made a point, year after year, of beseeching her to give up and undertake another sphere of like labor; and this annual temptation became almost a joke with her friends.

Her work was in no sense confined to the four walls of the Nursery. A large number of the children were of Italian parentage, and she soon came to take particular interest in their welfare. She always held that in many ways they were the most satisfactory people to deal with, and her last Easter at the Nursery she signalized her interest in them by giving a set of vases to the mission of San Salvatore.

The Italian colony soon came to know her, and no matter what hour of the night she appeared among them she was never molested. Once she happened on a crowd in that quarter, and would have been insulted by an intoxicated man, had not some cried out, "That is Miss Wiltse!" and way was instantly made for her.

She was much amused at the attitude of a certain Italian family towards her, who one would have thought had good cause to dread and fear her. A child of this family, hardly more than a baby, was missed from the Nursery for several days, and Mary, suspecting the truth, made her way late at night to the fruit-stall kept by the father, and there found the little thing in attendance. She at once informed the proper authorities, and the father was fined. The same thing happened a second time, and again Mary interfered, and the father was fined, this time heavily. But no amount of fines could shake the man's respect for Miss Wiltse, and all the while he was waging his little war against law and order, his youngest baby was kept in the Nursery at his request!

Though particularly fond of the Italians, her little world was exceedingly cosmopolitan in its make-up. Nor did she ever, on account of race or creed, refuse entrance for any child claiming her love and interest. By the very peculiarity of her position, she was nearest the great mass of the sorrowing, and came in closest relations with them. And truly enough was it said of her after her death, that the blessings of a great number of Christ's poor attended her.

She was an "unvested sister"[1] from

1 It is interesting to call to mind in this connection Miss Wiltse's intention to become a Deaconess; in her case one must think the crown, rather than the prophecy of a consecrated life.

choice, relying on the good purpose in her heart for sufficient protection. Neither was her courage often daunted, nor her quick wit overcome by obstacles. Called one night to see a sick child in a dangerous neighborhood, she found the stairway blocked by a drunken mob. Knowing the uselessness of attempting to pass through, she descended into the street and made her way to the third story from the outside by the fire escape. The astonishment of the sick child's mother may well be imagined. Her presence of mind the following incident will show : One night, sitting alone in the parlor, the front door having been left carelessly open, she heard a step behind her, and looking up saw a strange man. He reeled towards her in a drunken swing, and as he did so, she seized his arm and pushed him forward, saying, "Go out ; how dare you come in here !" "Of course," she said afterwards, "I was horribly frightened, but at the same time could hardly help laughing outright at the meek way he obeyed me. I finally got him to the door and pushed him into the street, and when I had locked and bolted myself in, did not know whether to laugh or cry."

Mention was made of the method by which she carried on her work. It was not a method guided by rule, but one adapting itself to circumstances and exigency. It has been said that, her day's work ended, she would often spend long evenings ministering to the sick children at their own homes. The Nursery itself was no less a refuge, "after hours," time and again, for many a wretched and desponding woman. "One cold day in December a particularly respectable woman with a baby in her arms came to the Nursery, seeking a home for her child. Her story was a sad and common one. She had been cruelly wronged, and was without home or friends. She was directed to several places where it was thought that the child might be taken, but in the evening she returned, having searched New-York in vain. A bed was prepared for her, but for a long time after she had retired she was heard sobbing bitterly. She was assured that everything would be done to help her, and that the child would be cared for until a home was found. 'I am not crying for that,' she exclaimed, 'but because you are so good to me.' The welcome she had received, coming after so cruel an experience of coldness and indifference, broke her down, and it was long before she could control her emotion. The next day a home was found for both herself and child."

These illustrations might be multiplied, but they are sufficient to indicate the character of her work and its varied outgrowths. They show it particularly in its threefold development: the care of the children, the interest taken in the life of their parents, and what might be called the "rescue work" in which she found herself every now and then engaged, owing to her overflowing sympathy.

The case of the wretched woman, the baptism of whose children Mary insisted upon against their mother's will, is a striking example of the relation she believed she must hold to her young charges. To her mind, their own mother had forfeited all natural claim upon them, and, in the providence of God, she herself was called to act as if the mother had been dead. She did not need, though it was welcome enough when it came, that mother's dying blessing upon her, to confirm her in the belief that she had acted rightly.

Again and again she had to decide such questions of grave responsibility alone, and it may safely be said that they were never decided otherwise than in relation to a principle, never hastily, never without calm forethought, never in obedience to a whim.

That she was often deceived in the estimate she put upon this or that woman's character with whom her work brought her in relation, is in no way strange. She but shared the bitter experience that is the inevitable lot of all such workers. Her confidence was only too often misplaced, her zeal and love repaid with base ingratitude.

It is difficult for one who was privileged to know her intimately to write of her otherwise than in a strain of high eulogy. Yet she had her special temptations to grapple with ; temptations peculiar to one of her ardent, impulsive, strong personality. She suffered agonies from an over-sensitiveness which, try as she would, she could not wholly overcome. It is true, also, that at times she manifested an imperious impatience towards criticism of, and what seemed like interference with, her methods of work, which often repulsed those who did not know her well.

She had, too, a certain jealous fear of division of labor, which was but the obverse side of her intense devotion. She preferred that the work in its entirety should be the expression of but one mind, and she paid dearly for her indulgence in what proved again and again a waste of what might otherwise have been a husbanded vitality. But it is doubtful if the work would have had more than a commonplace excellence, had she not transfused and transfigured each detail with her own ardent individuality.

She was peculiarly jealous of the children's love. A friend remembers once taking in his arms a little child (whose name will recall a host of happy hours in which she figured as supreme pet and joy), and, pointing to Miss Wiltse, saying, "Beatrice, you do not love Mama Wiltse as much as you do me, do you?" With what a cry of triumph, which had a pathetic ring in it, did Mary clasp the child, whose arms, outstretched to her, proved to whom her little love was given.

He remembers too, on the eves of three successive Christmas festivals, saying to Miss Wiltse: "You are tired out, and if you will let me, I will dress the tree for you." At the hour appointed, he came, but only to be met with the remark, "The tree is dressed, and everything is done!" Never did she begrudge a labor spent on her children's behalf. Nothing she could do herself would she permit others to do for them. What a succession of pictures so full of beauty and spontaneous life, so *uninstitutional*, one who knew her work well could call up! None lovelier than that which chance visitors at Grace House opposite might see who, at dusk, all unknown to her, had a glimpse of the babies' Nursery. The tension of the day's work was relaxed ; in a little time the mothers would come for their babies, but, until the last was taken, she remained there sitting in their midst, laughing and crooning over them,

Idle with love for her family !

At Far Rockaway, where she had them with her night as well as day, residents in the neighborhood of the house used to listen with delight to the evening hymns, sung as they gathered about her after supper, when the youngest children had been put to bed. Of one of these very youngest a pathetic story is told. It was Mary's custom, after the little ones had been put to bed, to kiss each child "good-night." A stran-

66

ger to the others and to the Nursery had been sent down from New-York, and when the tall figure bent over her she reached up her arms saying, "No one ever kissed me good-night before." What a world of motherless days and lonely childhoods such a sad little saying reveals.

To avoid confusion of thought it may be well to remind the reader again that the Nursery gathered to itself not only the very youngest babies, but children the oldest of whom were twelve years of age. These older girls and boys went to day-school in the neighborhood, returning at noon and at three o'clock. Most of them had been brought to the Nursery when young children and had remained ever since. This older portion formed what came to be called the Chantry choir. Strangers to New-York and the church found few sights more interesting than that of the little band who day by day, from October to June, led the singing at Evening Prayer. During Lent, when the services are held in the church itself, the children sang on Monday and Friday only; but with that exception their attendance and that of Miss Wiltse was rarely interrupted. The teaching of the children their hymns and chants devolved upon Mary, and the *repertoire* of the little ones was astonishingly large. Reference has been already made to the service in the oratory of the Nursery, so sweet, and happy, and sincere; but it is doubtful if the children ever had more delighted listeners than the sick at Bellevue. One of the chaplains of that hospital, the Rev. H. St. G. Young, her devoted and sincere friend, used at stated intervals to beg her to lend herself and her choir for a service in the wards, and she, wearied though she might be with the week's work, rarely refused. It was an hour of unalloyed happiness to the poor sufferers. On one occasion their singing awoke a sick man from his sleep, and he murmured to those near him: "I thought I had been in heaven." From bed to bed she passed with her little flock, saying a kind word, and giving a warm pressure of the hand.

She always refused to teach the children hymns other than those of the Church. "They can just as easily be taught good hymns and good tunes as the wretched jingles that are so popular," she used to insist; and who does not wish that such an example could prove contagious? It was now and then objected that the incongruity was painful when the little ones sang "O Paradise" and "Jerusalem, my happy home," and hymns of like nature. But for those familiar with her method of pointing the lesson of the hymns as of the prayers, there existed no such difficulty. She trusted—how often has she said it—

that sometime in the years to come, when no longer in the shadow of their Nursery home, the remembrance of some prayer said, some hymn sung, might be to her children as light on a dark way. Therefore she was anxious that with everything that was best and most elevated these, their earliest years, might be associated.

Her keen sense of humor came strongly to her aid in enabling her to distinguish between teaching suitable and unsuitable for the children. On one occasion she was taken to hear a preacher during an Advent mission who was widely advertised as a successful speaker to children. She never could refer to that address without a peal of laughter. "He knew nothing about them," she said, "and it was with difficulty I could keep from laughing outright in church. Not a word of what he was saying could the children understand." Rare indeed is that gift which she found so conspicuously lacking in this instance, and nothing delighted her more than to find some one who possessed it. She was particularly pleased with the Christmas talk given the Nursery children by their rector in 1888, and referred to it often as a model of what such talks should be. It was a presentation of the picture of the Shepherd and the lambs on the Judean hills; simple enough in itself, and, on that account, capable of apprehension by almost the youngest children. I refer to it because her appreciation of it was a key to her own teaching, a teaching enforced and enlightened by concrete examples rather than abstract statements.

A child's death was her opportunity for a little talk on Paradise, and how marked and intense grew the quiet, as she explained why a familiar face was no longer to be seen on earth, and how some day they would see it again in that Heavenly

Nursery. The baptism of a baby was made an object lesson more potent and lasting than a multitude of talks. Every spring it was her custom, in the presence of the children, to plant a few beans in a box of ivy, near the front window. Eagerly, as Easter approached, the children watched the tiny shoots as they found their way up through the mellow soil. The day came when the pod fell away and the new bean was discovered. Then, deftly and subtly, she pointed the Resurrection lesson, how in time the old body shall fall away, and the new, fresh, pure and sweet, rise in the presence of God. What child who ever saw that picture and heard her words can forget the lesson so exquisitely taught?

Fragmentary as are these recollections, culled from a multitude that might easily be set forth, they may suffice to witness to the truth of our estimate of a life both rare and noble.

They recall nearly eleven years of untiring and all but incessant labor in the service of the Nursery. Twice only, after Grace House-by-the-Sea was opened, did Miss Wiltse give over to another the charge of her summer's work. The end of such a life when it came could not but come suddenly.

A few months before she left the Nursery she had a dream which told plainly enough in what direction her thoughts and fears were running. She seemed to be lying in a wide, open space filled with a great thrilling light. "I seemed to hear," she said, "a voice saying to me, 'Mary, the Master is come, and calleth for thee.' And I replied, 'Tell Him I cannot come now, my work is not finished.'" When she told of it the next day, she said, with a smile: "I think I shall not go just yet." But within the year the voice she had seemed to hear had called her home. During the

73

summer of 1889, against the best wishes of her friends, she decided to take up her old place at Far Rockaway, and the record of those weeks was one of physical pain and suffering. Upon her return in the fall, the gravity of her condition was made known by a series of severe illnesses culminating in her physician's decision that an absolute change was indispensable. At Christmas, for it seemed almost impossible for her to get away, she insisted on leaving her sick bed to play for the children at their festival. "I think she knew," said one of her friends, "it was for the last time." The difficulty of getting some one to take her place during her absence seemed for a long time insurmountable. "I will be willing to go if Miss —— can come," she said, when the name of a devoted friend was mentioned; and when she heard that that had been arranged, she made her preparations to go. Late in January, 1890, she left Grace Memorial for the Adirondacks. What that day was for her no one will ever know, but the few letters from which extracts follow show how tenderly all her thoughts hovered about the home she had left, as the event proved, forever.

On the eve of her departure, she wrote to her most constant and loving friend, Mrs. George S. Bowdoin:

What can I say to you all? My heart is so full that sometimes I think I cannot stand it all. I have suffered so long and so much, and now to go away and leave everything I have worked so long for, and those who have become so dear to me, almost breaks my heart. With all that God has called me to suffer, what would it have been but for the tender sympathy and love which has come to me from my friends.

An extract from a letter written from the Adirondacks will show why so soon she left the mountains for her own home:

February 5, 1890.

I was glad to hear from you yesterday, and I feel encouraged. To-day I sat outdoors for two hours as a beginning. Imagine the change to me from an atmosphere of 75° to one at zero. The air is crisp and dry and I have no doubt that when I get accustomed to it I shall improve. . . . . I hope everything will go right at the Nursery. I am there in spirit all the time.

A few days later her friends heard she was back in Sing Sing. The change had come too late, and she determined not to be tempted away from home, but, if it were possible, to rest and recuperate.

She wrote on the 17th February from Sing Sing :

I am still alive, which, after the experience of the past two or three weeks, is a surprise. . . . . I do not know where I shall go next. I must gain a little strength and feel better before taking another trip. Oh, what a hard fight to gain what was so easily lost !

At home though she was, her constant thoughts were with her work, and all her letters are tinged with her eager interest about it. A few days later she wrote her friend in charge at the Nursery:

Mrs. Bowdoin tells me Mrs. Clark's baby is dead. You must not worry about it. I am sure you will do everything in your power for the children when they are sick, and if the Good Shepherd takes the little lambs to himself it is all right. . . . I am feeling better. I cough but little. . . . Has Mrs. Reynolds had her baby christened? It was to have been done before I left. Now will very likely be a sick time among the babies. . . . How much I think about it all, and how well I know what an anxiety it is.

Later, she wrote the same:

As for the children's Easter music, they never sing anything else in the church save the Easter anthem, but I should like them to learn the hymn " Jesus lives." They also know the Gospel for the day and the collect. The Gospel I think Dr. H—— will have them say in the church at this festival. If it should be mild and warm at Easter they can wear their white sun-bonnets, which are in the store-room.

The shadow of the inevitable was falling upon her, but it in no way terrified her. The friend to whom she wrote the following letter once said, "I cannot associate the thought of death with so strong a nature and personality as hers." It was equally difficult for her to imagine that the time had come when she must lay by at least "her active service."

"I wish," she wrote on March 20th,

"I might say better things of myself, but for the past winter it has been all down hill, and I am painfully conscious of the fact that I am daily growing weaker and suffering more. . . . I try to be patient and say it is all right, but sometimes when I find myself so powerless and know how much there is to be done I am disposed to be rebellious. But God knows best. He has tried me in active service, and now comes the "standing and waiting." I miss my work and my children, but am thankful everything goes so well. How rejoiced I am that Edith is trying to do so well, and is going to take a good step forward. I only pray that it may be the beginning of a true Christian life. I wish I might be with you all at Easter. Even though I am in my own home, surrounded by old and true friends, my heart longs for the work that has become so near and dear to me."

Daily did her children, too, remember her at their morning office, and the prayer that their rector had taught them to say was never forgotten:

Most Merciful Father, who art ever ready to listen to thy children's prayers, care tenderly, we beseech thee, for the absent head of the household and mother of this Nursery. Sustain her in weakness, comfort her when she is lonely, cheer her under discouragement, and, of thy great mercy, give her back to us in health and strength, for the love of thy dear Son, our Saviour, Jesus Christ. Amen.

How pathetically difficult it was to explain to the children, when the end came, why they were not again to look upon the face of her for whom they had prayed.

To them, from whom all these years she had never before been separated, she wrote, as well as to Matilda, a faithful co-worker, and one of their nurses:

MY DEAR LITTLE CHILDREN: How glad I am to hear that you are such good children. You do not know how happy it makes me to hear you are obedient, and try to give Matilda as little trouble as possible. I think of you a great deal, and will be so happy when I can come back to you again. You will help me to get well by trying to do everything right, and being good children. Those are very pretty verses Matilda taught you, and I hope you are listening when she is trying to teach you. See how many nice things you will know when I come home again to you! I have no dear children here; only a big white cat that jumps on my lap and would like to eat all my dinner and supper. So, you see, the children are the best. I am sure *my* children are, and one thing they may be very certain of, that no one loves them better than their

MAMA WILTSE.

MY DEAR MATILDA: I am only going to write you a short letter, as I am not feeling very well. This is a very beautiful country, but bitterly cold, and, I am afraid, will not agree with me. I am weaker than when I left home. I am so glad to have things go on well with you all. I do hope the children will be good, and not give you any more trouble than is really necessary. It will be such a comfort, and such a help, to me, if everything will go smoothly. No one will ever know how hard it is for me to go away and leave everything that is so dear to me. Sometimes I think I cannot do it, and then I must remember that the same loving hand which always gave me my health and strength has now seen fit to take them from me. I must bear it as patiently as possible. Give my love to all the dear children. There are not many minutes in the day that they are not in my thoughts. God bless and keep you all, is the constant prayer of your friend,

MARY WILTSE.

I hope the children will remember to say the collect for next Sunday, which will be Quinquagesima Sunday. It is one of my favorite collects.

MY DEAR MATILDA: I was very glad to get such nice letters from you. You need not be afraid about writing good English, for I am sure it was all right, and perfectly plain to me.

I have written a letter to the younger children in your room, which you will please read to them. How I do long to see you all. The time seems very long. Some days I am better, and many days I suffer a great deal. But I must try and be patient, and God, in his own good time, will, I trust, give me my health again. I hope the children are good, and that things will go right. Dear little Allie sent me such a nice letter. I will write to her soon. Tell Jeannette she should write to me. I think so much about all, every hour in the day. I am so very glad that Edith is doing well and going to take a good step for the future. May God watch over and protect you all and spare us to be united once more.

In one of the letters to Matilda she inclosed a little slip upon which she had written these words:

Three things for the children to remember and try to do every day in Lent:

Be obedient,

Be truthful,

Be gentle and kind.

Pray to God for help to do this, and you will be happy yourselves and make every one around you happy.

Of course the children wrote her continually, but no letter could have touched her more than this, which we cannot forbear to quote:

NEW-YORK, March 22, 1890.

DEAR MISS WILTSE: I am very sorry that you are sick, but I hope to see you well again. I pray to God day and night to make you better, and also my little brother Antonio and my little sister Mary pray for you. I am a very good girl in school. I am very anxious to see you in good health again. I let you know that everybody in the Nursery are well. I think I said enough, and I am

Yours truly,

ROSY CRISPANO.

Expressed by Rosy Crispano.

Written by Philip Crispano.

Under this quaint little letter is the picture of a flower-basket and the legend attached :

May your Easter be as bright as these flowers.

That Easter was indeed to be bright, but with the first faint gleam of a light that "never was on sea or land."

The memory of those last few days is a sacred and peculiar heritage to those nearest and dearest to her. On Good Friday, suffering agonies as she was, she whispered, "One ought to be glad to suffer on the day upon which our Lord was crucified."

On the afternoon of Easter Day her friend and Bishop knelt by her bed, and she repeated with him happily and calmly the Lord's Prayer. By her side stood a lily the children had sent her, and opposite her bed hung a crayon of the little Beatrice she had so dearly loved.

At that same hour the Nursery choir were singing their Easter carols in the great church, and they who loved her and them, knowing how swiftly they were to be bereaved, found the message of the day take on a deeper meaning.

Early on the morning of the following Tuesday, the 8th of April, she passed quietly away.

AN UNVESTED SISTER

BY

THE RT. REV. H. C. POTTER, D. D.

BISHOP OF NEW-YORK

AN UNVESTED SISTER.

IN the autumn of 1879 the rector of a New-York parish found himself in an unusual dilemma. A munificent friend and parishioner had placed at his command some $75,000 for a *Crèche*, or Day Nursery, on the model of the admirable institutions in France for the care of infants and very young children while their mothers were absent at day's work. An association to supervise and sustain the work had been organized under the leadership of a lady of rare ability and devotion, and a beginning had already been made.

But, as so often, it was found that zeal, money, compassion, were not enough to secure success. Most of all, there was needed a competent head. One after another was tried and withdrew from a task at once delicate, difficult, and unwonted; and the friends of the enterprise were beginning to be perplexed and disheartened.

At this juncture there came one day a visitor who brought with her a letter of introduction which, from its source and its terms, compelled both attention and respect; and as he to whom it was addressed laid it down, he could not but hope that he had found the instrument he was in search of. The bearer, however, seemed little more than a young girl, was singularly reserved in speech, confessed to her inexperience in the particular enterprise contemplated, and, while refusing to be lavish in promises, said simply and quietly that she should like to try the work, and would not spare herself in the doing of it.

She never did. A mere experiment when she put her brave, firm hand to it, it grew under that hand like a strong and well-watered plant. Grateful for every better convenience and every larger opportunity for her task, she never clamored for the one nor complained of the lack of the other. Both came by a sort of silent and resistless compulsion. It was impossible to deny to such a woman the means for her ministry, for she made it at once absolutely preëminent for its character and range. Steadily, as the years went by, it grew and widened. The handful of children became a score, and the score well nigh an hundred. "Grace House-by-the-Sea" came to answer the demand that the winter's work should somehow go on during the summer. The potent spell over the babies and little children reached out and touched, and drew, and held, the mothers. The swift insight, the absolute sincerity, the inexhaustible sympathy, brought to her door young girls and young wives, fathers and brothers, representing every grade of penury, wretchedness, and misfortune. She became to a wide neighborhood counselor, banker, arbitrator, comforter, nurse, physician. By day and night she went everywhere, and ministered in the hiding-places of sorrow and shame, empanoplied in her strong, single, utterly self-forgetting purpose. Nothing daunted her; nothing made her despair. She had no illusions about evil, and she looked all that she had to see straight in the face. But, with this absolute candor, with an often impatience of mere sentiment which, like that of Sister Dora (whom in many rare and noble traits she singularly resembled), broke out sometimes in vigorous speech, she combined an inextinguishable tenderness that never wearied and never drew back. Broken-hearted creatures fled to her, out of some horror of infamy, at dead of night, and were sheltered, soothed, admonished, and loved, through all their falterings and stumblings till, like him at the Beautiful Gate, they could arise and stand upright on their feet. Children turned to her with that sure and unerring instinct that never mistakes the affectation of interest for its reality, and clung to her skirts as a shelter and a refuge from all sorrows. Herself neither wife nor mother, she disproved anew the silly fallacy that only a mother's heart can know a child's griefs. Resolute, almost brusque sometimes, dominant and sovereign by original endowment, she yet carried within her a child's heart; and the time never came, no matter how long the day nor how sore the strain, when the one incomparable privilege of her life was not to have her little ones clamoring at her knees for her recognition and caress.

In a household of nearly a hundred very little children, wayward, undisciplined, flashing into flame, often, with the hot blood of Spanish or Italian or Irish ancestry (for she gathered all nations within her fold), it could not but be that sometimes the air was turbulent and stormy. And then it was a spectacle once witnessed never to be forgotten, to see her enter a room vibrant almost to bursting with the tumultuous disorder, and, without raising her voice, hush the whole tempest into a stillness in which there was never one slightest element of terror or of mere surrender to physical force, but a swift and eager acquiescence in a rule as tender as it was strong, and as patient as it was inflexible.

Such a character may, perhaps, be possible, without the ennobling spring of a strong and steadfast Christian faith, but the question is alien to this illustration of it, for, from first to last, such a faith was the corner-stone of the whole superstructure. The qualities that in Sister Dora made her impatient of cant, as she was of mere sentiment, were in Mary Wiltse as marked as in her English sister. She was not voluble about religious things, nor religious feelings. She had the characteristic reserve, in these regards, that marks a healthy Anglo-Saxon nature. But, in the dear little oratory where, morning and evening, she was wont to gather her untamed brood about her, and where she was at once organist, choir master, and chaplain, in the clear, steadfast conviction which shone in her of the nearness of that Divine Presence on which she leaned, and in whose strength she wrought, her wayward flock learned first to be reverent, and then obedient and devout, and then, as some one has put it, "clear-sighted toward God," until, as was with her, the earthly Nursery and the Heavenly Paradise opened into each other—so it came to be with them.

It was impossible that one so deep in the spirit of her work, and so ceaseless in the expenditure of her strength and her affections in the doing of it, should stand a strain so exhausting. Once and again she owned, with characteristic reluctance, however, what it "took out" of her. But, though she had nearest to her in the direction of it those who saw what its end must be, and though the friend and associate in its oversight upon whom she chiefly leaned besought her from time to time to give herself some temporary respite from it, she could not bring herself to do so. At long intervals she took what she called a vacation, but she was always unhappy till it was ended.

And so, all the more swiftly drew on the *long* vacation. She saw it come, and faced it without a tremor. "I am sorry to leave my work," she said, "but it is all right"; and then "fell on sleep." To one who, as the end came, sought to reassure her, she said, with the old, resolute, transparent tone that rang so clear to the last: "Do you think I am afraid?" She spoke of Paradise, and the loving ones who peopled it, as if she knew beforehand how surely she would be at home in her Father's House, and, as she said, "among my babies."

They came—those among the living who were old enough—to the home of her childhood, and stood about her bier, and sang the hymns that she had taught them: "O Paradise, O Paradise," "Jesus, tender Shepherd, hear me," and the rest— the tears streaming down their little cheeks, but no voice faltering, no smothered sob breaking the even cadence— "just as she would have wished," as they knew and said—the calm command of that strong and tender heart reaching out of her coffin, and ruling and leading to the last. And then the Church spoke its words of immortal promise and hope, her true friend and pastor,[1] who honored her for her work's sake, repeating, with the children, the *Credo*, which she had taught them, and commending them in tender words to their Father and hers; and when the last words within the Church's walls were said, those who loved her best accompanied her to the quiet God's acre hard by, and there, among the trees, and birds, and flowers that she loved so well, with the sun flooding with light the grave that sloped so gently towards its westering rays, we left her tired form to rest. Life, as most men count life, had given her little, and cost her much. But one has said: "He that findeth his life shall lose it; and he that loseth his life for my sake, shall find it again." And she knows now that "he saith true."

1 The Rev. Dr. W. R. Huntington.

CPSIA information can be obtained
at www.ICGtesting.com
Printed in the USA
BVHW04*1219210918
528171BV00010B/444/P

9 780484 58369